With love to my big brother, Doug—the best brother, father,
grandfather, and great-grandfather a family could have!
—Kathy Lawrence

Dedicated to my grandchildren and their children and so on . . .
and to all who have ever asked, "Heavenly Father, are You really there?"
—Janice Kapp Perry

Text © Janice Kapp Perry

Artwork on pages 2, 5, 6, 9, 14, 17, 21, 26, and 32 © Kathy Lawrence by
arrangement with The Ansada Group, LLC Sarasota, FL.
Artwork on pages 10, 18, 22, 25, 29, and 30 © Jean Monti,
courtesy of The Greenwich Workshop, Inc., www.greenwichworkshop.com.

Front cover image: *The Lord's Blessing* © Kathy Lawrence
Back cover image: *On the Beach* © Jean Monti
Cover and interior designed by Christina Marcano
Cover design copyright © 2013 by Covenant Communications, Inc.
Published by Covenant Communications, Inc.
American Fork, Utah

Printed in China
First Printing: September 2013

19 18 17 16 15 14 13   10 9 8 7 6 5 4 3 2 1

ISBN: 978-1-62108-127-2

Heavenly Father, are you really THERE?

AND
do you hear *and*
answer
every
CHILD'S
PRAYER?

SOME say that HEAVEN is FAR away,

Heavenly Father, I remember now

SOMETHING THAT **JESUS** told disciples LONG AGO:

"Suffer the CHILDREN to come to ME."

Father, in prayer I'm coming NOW to thee.

You are His child;

His **L**ove now SURROUNDS *you.*

Jean Monti ©

OF SUCH is the KINGDOM

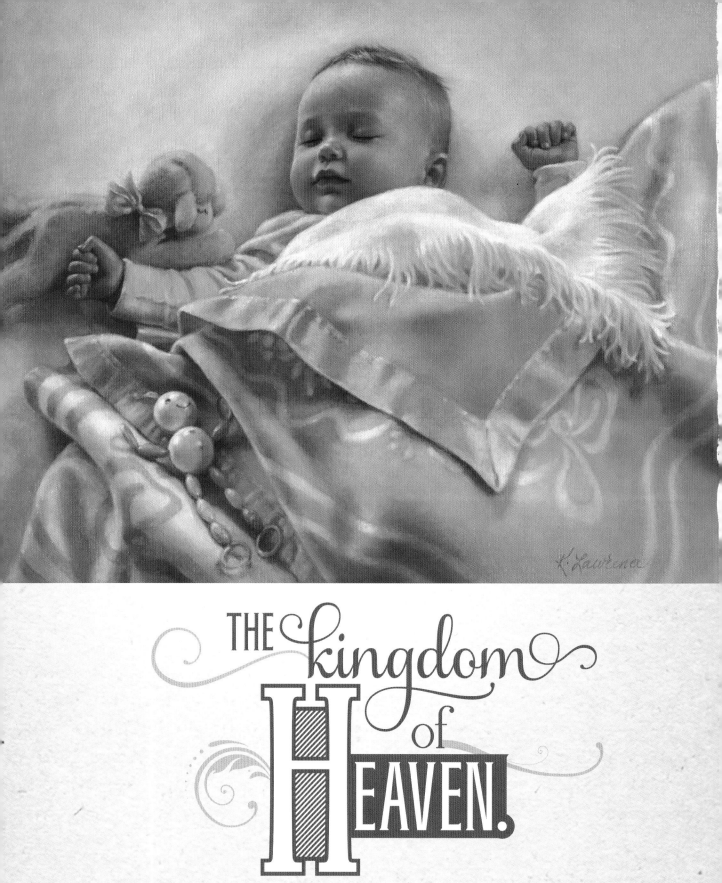

THE *kingdom* of HEAVEN.

Art Credits

A Child's Prayer

Reverently ♩ = 63–69
Sing parts separately, then combined.

1. Heav - en - ly Fa - ther, are you real - ly there? And do you hear and an - swer ev - 'ry child's____ prayer? Some say that heav - en is far a - way, But I feel it

2. Pray, he is there; Speak, he is lis - t'ning. You are his child; His